CONTENTS

A SPIDER FOR TEA

and other stories

Gordon Volke

RAVETTE PUBLISHING

Cover Design by John Forshaw
Line Drawings by David Boulter

Printed and bound in Great Britain
for Ravette Publishing Limited,
Unit 3, Tristar Centre,
Star Road, Partridge Green,
West Sussex RH13 8RA
by Cox & Wyman Ltd, Reading, Berkshire

ISBN: 1 84161 036 4

FOREWORD

Originally, this book was called 'Captive Audience' and was designed to be read aloud in Middle School assemblies, but, like all good stories, the characters and situations grew in the telling and it soon became clear that the adventures of Jo and her friends had a much wider appeal. These stories of ten-year-olds behaving like teenagers can be read alone by anyone from eight to eighty!

Yet, at the same time, the original intention remains. School assemblies are almost the only time you find a large body of children together in one place, waiting to listen. It's a great opportunity (often missed) to create an exciting, funny, or moving moment, mutually shared. Let's hope that, somewhere or sometime, a story from 'Old Grumpus' or 'A Spider For Tea' creates just such a moment.

POPPER
PAMPERS
SMALL
TODDLER
TALES.

A SPOT OF BABYSITTING

Mark Parsons asked me out the day after he dumped Denice. We were on our way out to play rounders against the teachers when he said,

"Do you want to go out with me?"

"Yes," I replied - and that was it!

Normally, I'm pretty hot at rounders. My Mum showed me how to stand sideways and step forward as you hit the ball, getting all your body weight behind it. If you make contact, it goes for miles! Not today, though. Either I was excited, or not concentrating, or both, but I just sliced the ball up into the air, giving a dolly-drop catch to Mr Weatherly. For a split second, I hoped he'd drop it - perhaps on purpose, like my Dad used to do when I was little –

but no such luck. This was a proper match and I was out. Part of me felt very miffed, but, as I reasoned with myself, the one person I always tried to impress, didn't need impressing any more!

"So where's Lover Boy going to take you on your first date?" asked Fran, as we walked home together after school.

"I don't know," I said. "The pictures?"

"The pictures!" echoed Fran, screwing up her freckled face in contempt. "People don't go to the pictures these days. They go clubbing."

"We're only ten, Fran!" I exclaimed.

"Pictures it is, then," she laughed. "What are you going to see?"

"I don't know," I repeated.

"Doesn't matter, eh?" chuckled Fran, nudging my shoulder. "So long as you're in the back row with Mark's arm round you, playing tonsil-tennis."

"Don't be disgusting!" I cried.

"Sorry," said Fran. "He needn't have his arm round you!"

In fact, Mark didn't speak to me again until the last day of term. I'd just got in after a long and tedious afternoon. We'd been allowed to take in games, which always bored me rigid, and then we'd had this really long assembly. Anyway, the phone rang and it was Mark.

"You doing anything this evening?" he asked.

"No," I replied.

"Fancy a spot of babysitting?" he asked.

"Babysitting!" I exclaimed.

"It'll be fun, Jo," he urged, using my name for the first time. "My sister's got this two-year-old who sleeps right through. She's also got a big house. We can watch TV, play pool, order a pizza - and we'll be on our own."

"We're not old enough for this, Mark," I said. "We need babysitters ourselves!"

"My Dad'll be there, too," added Mark.

"Then how are we going to be on our own if your Dad's there?" I asked.

"He'll be upstairs, decorating," explained Mark. "We won't see him."

It sounded a bit of a mess to me, but I didn't say anything. I was scared that if I turned him down, Mark wouldn't ask me again, so I said, "Okay, then. You're on!"

It seemed a terribly long time between putting the phone down and Mark calling round to collect me. I tried on several outfits, eventually deciding on my red mini skirt with a green and yellow t-shirt.

"Too dressy for babysitting," advised Fran on the phone. "Besides, you'll look like a traffic-light!"

So I changed into an ordinary jumper and jeans and went downstairs to tell mum. Surprisingly, for once, she did not mind. She'd known Mark's mum for a long time.

"I'll be pleased if you're friends with them," she said. "They're nice people."

For once in her life, mum was right. I warmed to Mark's dad the moment I met him.

"So you're the famous Jo we've heard so much about," he said, holding open the car door for me.

"Yes," I replied lamely, feeling myself blush.

"Taken you two long enough to get together ..." he continued.

"Dad!" interrupted Mark sharply. "Shut up!"

"Yessir!" said Mr Parsons, saluting. "Sorry, sir!"

I felt like a film star sitting in the back of the big, posh car with Mark. And his sister's house was everything he had said it was. It had lovely carpets and curtains - not like my tatty house. Mark's dad marched straight upstairs to get on with his work.

His sister, who was in a hurry to get out, showed us where everything was and left. Suddenly, Mark and I were alone together.

I expected to feel strange and awkward, but I didn't. It just seemed right being with Mark.

We raided the fridge, sat down on the huge sofa with loads of nibbles and started channel-surfing. They had digital, so there were about fifty programmes to choose from. In our house, that would be a recipe for endless arguments, but Mark and I both agreed on a nature documentary about big snakes and sat back to enjoy it. I knew he was going to put his arm around me before he even did it. I snuggled onto his shoulder and waited. Any moment now, he was going to kiss me.

This was a moment I had waited for since First School. Mark had always been the one for me and here I was, at last, about to kiss him. It would be my first proper kiss with a boy. Eddie had given me a peck goodnight once, but that didn't count. This was going to be the real thing. Mark turned his head towards me and, for a second, I could smell his breath. It felt wildly exciting. Then his lips brushed mine and ...

"WAAAAHH!" I heard. "WAAAAHHH!

WAAAAAHHH!"

"Ignore it," whispered Mark, trying to continue.

"Ignore what?" I asked.

Then Mr Parsons put his head round the door.

"Baby's crying!" he said.

It felt unreal as I got off the sofa and followed Mark upstairs to the baby's bedroom. The big moment hadn't happened and it didn't look as if it would now, because the baby was wide awake. He was called Tristan and, the moment he saw us, he stopped crying and started rattling the sides of his cot. It was obvious he wanted to get out of it. He brushed aside the mug of milk that Mark gave him and we had no choice but to take him downstairs with us.

"Your Dad'll know what to do," I said.

"No, he won't," replied Mark. "He's hopeless with kids!"

Mark, on the other hand, was very good with Tristan. He changed his nappy without too much trouble and managed to get him to drink some of the milk, but when we tried to get him back into his cot ... disaster! He screamed the house down.

"What's going on?" asked Mark's Dad,

peering round the door again.

"Tristan won't go back to sleep," I explained.

"You'll just have to play with him then," said Mr Parsons. "After all, babysitting isn't all eating, watching telly and snogging."

"Dad ...!" shouted Mark.

"I know," laughed Mr Parsons, disappearing upstairs again. "Shut up!"

Before long, the sitting-room looked like a bomb site. We took out all of Tristan's toys which he threw about, laughing happily all the time. Then he went round picking them up and giving them to us, one by one.

"This'll tire him out," chuckled Mark. But it didn't! If anything, the little rascal seemed to get more and more excited and lively. He started wandering off on his wobbly legs, trying to climb the stairs. We had to keep bringing him back, struggling and kicking, and then laughing gleefully as he went back again. On top of all this, Mark's dad came downstairs and flopped into one of the armchairs.

"Who's going to make me a nice cup of tea?" he asked.

I went in the kitchen, leaving Tristan

with the pair of them in the lounge. A football match was now on TV and I could hear from their excited shouts, that it was a good game. I made a big mug of tea for Mr Parsons and carried it gingerly in from the kitchen.

"Careful," I said, sounding just like my mother, "it's very hot."

"Thanks luv," beamed Mark's dad, taking a noisy slurp.

Mark was just filling me in on who was playing when I looked around.

"Where's Tristan?" I asked.

"He was over in the corner a moment ago," said Mr Parsons, casually.

"Well, he's not there now!" I said, a note of urgency creeping into my voice.

Could we find that toddler? He seemed to have disappeared into thin air!

"The doors and windows are all shut," said Mark, "so he can't have gone outside."

"Then he's in the house somewhere," continued Mr Parsons, "and we'd better find him - FAST!"

We looked in the cupboards and the larder. We looked in the bedrooms and the bathroom. We looked in toy boxes and laundry baskets, behind beds and chairs, under coats and duvets. Not a sign. We were starting to panic when we heard noises from the bedroom that was being decorated. We pushed open the door ... and there was Tristan, grinning from ear to ear, with one foot in a pot of white emulsion!

You have never seen such a mess in all your life! Mark's Dad had almost finished the room and was just touching up a corner of the ceiling. So the new blue wallpaper, the windows and some of the carpet, which wasn't covered up, were now plastered with white paint! It was like a bad dream - only it was real and suddenly we were getting the blame!

"You're supposed to be the babysitters!" shouted Mr Parsons. "Why didn't you keep an eye on him?"

"That's not fair, Dad!" retorted Mark. "Why didn't you keep out of the way? We were doing fine until you arrived."

It was a very different journey home that night. We had cleared up the best we could, but the room was ruined and would have to be decorated all over again. We had, however, managed to get Tristan down. To see him sleeping peacefully in his cot with a few splashes of white still on his face, you'd never have thought a littl'un like that could have caused so much chaos!

But Mr Parsons was cross, and Mark was upset about being shouted at in front of me, so the atmosphere in the car was pretty tense. That is, until I started to giggle.

I couldn't help it. Suddenly, everything about this evening - my first real date - seemed ridiculous and I started to laugh. The others soon followed suit and, in the end, Mr Parsons had to pull in for a while because he was laughing so much, he could not see where he was going. Eventually, we arrived outside my house.

"You've got five minutes, you two," he said, his eyes twinkling.

Mark walked me to my front door and we faced each other, ready to kiss again.

"THERE you are!" cried Mum, yanking open the door. "You said you'd be back about half eleven, but it's nearly one o'clock now."

"It's okay, Mum ... " I began.

"It's NOT okay!" insisted Mum. "I've been waiting up all this time, and I've got work tomorrow. Inside now please, madam."

I looked at Mark and shrugged my shoulders. He looked back and smiled. Obviously, it was not going to be, and our first kiss would have to wait for another day.

THE DONKEY RIDE

Families are funny, aren't they? Mine's okay - in parts. Mum and dad get on all right. Dad prefers me because I'm sporty. Mum prefers David because he's clever and good. David and I pretend to hate each other, but he always comes running to me with his problems and I suppose I love him, even though he's a boring, nerdy, four-eyed, tiresome little twit. Anyway, we all get along together when we're at home because we're out of each other's way. When we're all together - like on our annual summer holiday - then it's a different story. We turn into the family from Hell!

"Are we nearly there yet?" I asked, as we set off in the car and turned out of our street.

"Don't be silly, Joanna!" snapped mum.

"Only joking," I said, rolling my eyes.

"I thought it was funny," chuckled dad. "Like when you were little ... "

"Yes, dad," I interrupted, stopping him from stating the obvious any further.

"Don't be rude to dad," said David.

"You can shut up, you smelly little worm!" I exclaimed.

"STOPPIT!" shouted mum. "We're not having this all the way down to Devon!"

We did, of course. David and I, on the back seat, bickered and fought quietly about everything we could think of. Mum and I fell out when we stopped at a service station because I wanted to spend some of my holiday money and she said I should keep it. Then mum and dad quarrelled because dad insisted on sticking to the motorway, even though it was choc-a-bloc with holiday traffic.

"Why can't we go on the back roads?" grumbled mum. "It's got to be better than sitting in these queues."

"Because, my sweet," said dad,

"with you navigating, we'll probably end up in Scotland."

And that was it! Mum refused to speak any more and we all lapsed into silence, enduring the journey, which seemed to last a lifetime.

About seven o'clock, feeling stiff and a bit sick, we arrived at this little boarding house in Seaton. It was nice. The house was at the top of a steep hill that ran down to the sea, and the street was full of holidaymakers, looking happy and relaxed, strolling about in the warm evening light. I wanted to go exploring straight away, but mum said no.

"Supper and bed for you two," she ordered. "You can make a fresh start in the morning."

I couldn't be bothered to argue any more, so I did as I was told for once.

Next morning, sitting round the breakfast table, sipping orange juice (something we don't usually have at home), I felt excited and happy and bursting with energy.

"Can we go to the beach today?" I asked.

"No, thanks," said David. "The beach is boring!"

"Only if you're a wimp ... " I began, and stopped myself. I realised that arguing was unlikely to get me my own way. In the end, it was decided that dad would take me to the beach, while mum went round the shops with David. Then we'd all meet up for a picnic lunch on the pier.

Dad was a bit quiet as we walked down the hill to the beach, bags bulging with my football and swimming stuff. When we had a kick-about on the sand, his heart wasn't in it as usual, and he didn't do any of his fancy saves. Although he didn't say so, I reckon he'd had a drink or two at the bar the night before, to get over that awful drive. Doesn't suit him, my dad. He's a lightweight! Still, I didn't mind when he sat down in a deckchair and started to read his paper. I was glad to be free at last.

The sand was firm and moist down near the sea, so I set about building a sandcastle. Okay, I know it's a bit babyish, but at my age, you can make a really good one - the sort you can only dream about making when you're little.

I worked really hard in the hot morning sunshine and built a real beauty, turrets at each corner and a moat round the outside. Dad seemed to recover and helped me dig a trench down to the sea, so the moat filled with water. Then he went to the kiosk and bought some little flags for the turrets. They looked lovely, their bright colours flapping in the breeze. He also bought two big ice-creams with flakes in and we stood together, licking them and admiring our handiwork. I felt REALLY happy.

Then dad suggested a donkey ride.

"No thanks, dad," I said. "That really is for little kids."

"Oh go on, Jo," he urged, holding up his camera. "I promised mum I'd take some pictures and that would make a lovely snap."

"Oh, all right," I agreed, not wanting to be difficult on such a nice day.

I felt a bit self-conscious, towering over the other kids in the queue and it took ages before it was my turn, but eventually the wrinkled old donkey-man helped me onto a donkey called Mabel. She just stood there, weary and resigned, waiting to be led up and down the beach for the umpteenth time. I felt sorry for her and wanted to get off, but dad arrived with his camera and I was forced to sit up straight and smile.

Dad was still taking his last picture when it happened. A swarm of wasps, attracted by the apple cores and lollypop sticks in the nearby bin, buzzed down and sent everyone screaming in all directions. The noise frightened Mabel and one of the wasps must have stung her because, with a snort of rage, she shot off across the sands, with me still on her back!

It took me several moments to realise what was really happening. It felt like a silly dream ... or something out of a comedy film. But this was no joke! Here I was, hurtling along on a terrified, out-of-control donkey, with no-one there to help me, except myself!

"Whoa, Mabel!" I shouted, pulling firmly on the reins. It worked a bit and she started to slow down, but when I tried it again, my foot slipped out of one of the stirrups and I was forced to grab her mane to stay on. This scared the poor creature again and she carried on running, with me clinging on for dear life. I had just managed to pull myself back into the saddle when we reached the rocks at the end of the beach and Mabel threw me off! Luckily, I landed on my back in the sandy space between two rocks. It hurt, of course, particularly my left arm which I gashed on some barnacles, but I was okay. There was nothing broken.

I lay for a moment, listening to the roar of the sea to my left and the screeching cries of the gulls overhead. Then I got up and felt instantly light-headed. When I recovered, I saw Mabel trotting back along the beach, her reins trailing in the sand. She was already too far away for me to catch her, so I started to follow her, but I'd only taken a few steps when this huge wave came rolling in towards me and I had to scramble to one side over the rocks to avoid getting soaked. The roller was followed by another ... and another - and I realised that the tide was coming in.

"Help!" I shouted. "HELP! HELP!" Nobody answered, of course. I was all on my own down at this gloomy and rocky end of the beach. And I was in real danger of getting cut off by the incoming tide!

There was a small cave where the rocks joined the bottom of the cliffs and I was sorely tempted to shelter inside it and wait to be rescued, but I realised it would probably fill right up with water when the tide came in, so I'd be trapped. I decided the only thing to do was to clamber back over the rocks to the beach, beating the tide. But it wouldn't be easy. The rocks were slippery and sharp, and the sea was getting nearer by the minute. Then I looked behind me and saw that the rocks ran round a small headland.

"Yes!" I shouted, excitedly.

If I went round the headland, there was probably another beach which would be nearer and easier to reach.

It was the greatest mistake I'd ever made in my life! Rounding the headland, I saw that there wasn't another beach, just miles of seaweed-covered rocks leading to a sheer cliff-face. I had gambled ... and lost! And, for the first time, I realised that I probably wasn't going to get out of this nightmare. An hour ago, I was digging sandcastles and eating ice-cream with my dad. Now I was stuck in a desert of slime-covered rocks, about to be drowned or swept away by the ever-increasing waves.

There was only one way out - and that was up! I'd done some rock-climbing before at an Activity Centre I went to with the school, but that had been up a nice, smooth wall with a safety rope round my middle and a big, bearded instructor called Paul bellowing instructions up at me. This time, I was on my own with no help or equipment to support me. But danger - real danger - focuses your mind and gives you strength and determination you never knew you had. And so, realising to stay on the rocks and hope for the best meant curtains, I started climbing the cliffs.

The hardest bit was first. The sea had worn away the very base of the headland, so the rock was at an angle, rather than being straight up. It felt a bit like climbing the ceiling.

I used a great deal of effort to get started and I was already panting and sweating by the time it got a bit easier, with more footholds and handholds in the rockface. I thought I was doing well for a while, but then the cliffs became crumbly and I found myself causing miniature landslides every time I tried to grip. I was also starting to feel exhausted and realised I wouldn't make it to the top. It was much too far away.

For a while, I just stayed still, panting and gasping, clinging on like a spider. Then, just to the left, I spotted a ledge. It wasn't terribly big, but it would be enough for me to sit on - if it would take my weight. Inch by inch, I climbed across to it and, for once, my luck was in. The ledge was solid and I heaved myself onto it, sitting hunched up with my arms around my knees.

The view was spectacular! The sky and the sea met in a haze of summer blue and, below me, the tide had now covered the rocks and those big, Devon rollers were smashing against the cliffs in a frenzy of foam. Normally, I would have warmed to this scenery, but as you can imagine, the hugeness and unfriendliness of it all, scared me to death. I found myself thinking about Mark.

We'd made up for the lack of kisses on our first date, but we hadn't seen much of each other since. He'd been on holiday for a week and then, as soon as he came back, we had gone away. I'd promised to send him a postcard every single day. Didn't look as if that would happen now.

As time wore on, I began to feel cold and hungry. It was windy up here, perched on the cliffs like a seagull, and the sweat of my exertions had turned cold and uncomfortable. I tried to cheer myself up by singing songs, like in a film I once saw on TV one Sunday afternoon, but I soon got tired and gave up. I shouted for help a few times, but who was there to hear? And then I must have started to doze because I could hear drumming getting louder and louder, like a Drum 'n' Bass video on MTV.

"THAKKA-THAKKA-THAKKA!" it went. "THAKKA-THAKKA-THAKKA!"

Opening my eyes suddenly, I saw a rescue helicopter hovering at the top of the cliffs and a man on a rope descending towards me. He told me not to talk as he clipped a safety harness round me and I was pulled back up, clinging to him like a baby.

Mum, dad and David were already waiting for me as we landed at the helicopter base. I expected mum to be cross, as well as relieved, but she was all hugs and tears. After all, it wasn't my fault this had happened, was it? Poor dad looked as white as a sheet as he waited for his cuddle. He'd realised something was really wrong when Mabel had returned without me. Unable to find me or reach the end of the beach because of the tide, he'd phoned the coastguard, who had arranged for the chopper to be scrambled immediately. They soon spotted me with the help of their infra-red camera.

My family weren't the only ones at

the base. A TV news crew, who had been filming another story nearby, got wind of the rescue and filmed my dramatic return. That evening, I was on Sky News.

"Is there anything you'd like to say?" asked the reporter, before they whisked me off to hospital for a check-up.

"Yes," I replied. "I'd like to thank the people who rescued me. And I'd like to say Hi to Mark, my boyfriend at home."

That was a good idea, don't you think? Saved me having to send him a postcard!

LOST AND FOUND

Remember Old Grumpus? He said to me, after we'd got friendly, that being ten was the best time of your whole life. I didn't believe him at first - my little life always seems to be full of problems and worries. But now I knew what he meant.

It was the last two weeks of the summer holidays. The weather was good and Mark and I were together again, out playing from dawn 'til dusk, free as birds. No parents, no teachers, no real rules – we were free to go where we wanted and do what we wanted. It was wonderful. And I was grateful to Old Grumpus for making me aware of it.

These good times didn't last long, though. That big notice in Woolworths' window - BACK TO SCHOOL - acted like a warning which we all tried to ignore, but it soon came true.

Before I knew it, it was September and I was back in my scratchy old school skirt and woolly jumper. We were in Year Seven now, our final year at Middle School. I dreaded to think what it would feel like next year when were going up to the Comp.

The one thing that made going back to school bearable, was the prospect of being in Mr Matthews' class. He was a lovely teacher, everyone said so, and he had a soft spot for me because he ran the football team and I was the only girl he'd ever had in it. I wanted to work really hard for Mr Matthews, but I didn't get the chance. Fran was waiting for me on the first morning with shocking news.

"Matthews isn't coming back," she said.

"WHAT?" I almost shouted.

"He was taken ill on holiday," explained Fran. "He's okay, but he's retiring. We've got Mrs Fisher instead."

I felt a tear prickling the back of my eyes, but I fought it back.

"At least we can call her 'Fish-Face'," I joked bravely.

In fact, my nickname did not stick.

Our new teacher became known as 'The Old Trout' or just 'Trout'. It was a great name for her. She looked a bit like a trout and was almost as dull. I reckon there are two types of teachers - those that are human beings first and do their teaching as a job and those that are teachers all the time. 'Trout' was definitely the latter kind. She spoke like a teacher, thought like a teacher, even walked about like a teacher – every moment of the day. I bet she's just the same on a Saturday afternoon!

Mrs Fisher wasn't the only change to our class, either. We had a new boy called Darren Williams. He was cocky and arrogant, a bit like my old enemy Denice used to be before we made friends. I disliked him straight away, but Mark and the boys got on with him like a house on fire. He was very good at football, you see. They all spent every moment on the school field, kicking around in the autumn sunshine.

"How's Marky-Baby?" asked Fran, one long boring lunchtime.

"Never see him," I replied, wearily.

"Ahh," she teased. "Has Flash Daz taken him away from you?"

"Shut up, Fran!" I snapped.

With Mr Matthews gone, Mr

Weatherly took over the running of the football team. He held his first practice after school on Thursday and I went along. I wish I hadn't. Darren was there.

"What's she doing here?" he exclaimed, looking me up and down with a leer of contempt.

I expected Mark to say something, but it was Eddie who leapt to my defence.

"She's good, Dazzer," he said. "Plays in the team regular."

"But she's a girl!" scoffed Darren.

That made me see red. I stepped up to Darren so my face was close to his.

"So what?" I spat. "You big-headed, sexist pig!"

I didn't see Darren's fist, but I felt it hit me in the stomach. It hit me hard and I fell over backwards, startled and confused. The boys gathered round, chanting: "Fight! Fight!" and part of me felt strangely pleased that they were including me in one of their rituals. But I was frightened of Darren standing over me, looking ugly with aggression. Luckily, Mr Weatherly arrived at that moment and broke us up. I felt upset and angry, so I walked off.

"I don't want to play in this team," I shouted. "Have Superboy instead."

I kept out of Darren's way from then

on, but I could tell it wasn't over. Whenever we met, he glared at me or made a rude sign. He scared me - he was such a psycho. So I reverted to girlie things and took up skipping with Fran.

One morning play, I left our rope in my desk, so I asked the teacher on duty if I could nip inside and fetch it. She allowed me to and, as I hurried into the classroom, I thought I saw movement in the cloakroom outside, but I couldn't see anything. So I ignored it and grabbed the rope for our game. It was a good session. We got six jumping together at the same time until flat-footed Fran messed it all up!

We're supposed to have art on Tuesday afternoons, but the painting things weren't set out and, instead, the whole of Year Seven was marched into the hall for a special assembly. We had to wait while a dinner-lady swept up all the crisps and bits of sandwiches from lunchtime and then we sat down to be faced by a very grim-looking Mrs Horrocks, the headmistress.

"A very serious incident occurred at morning break," she said. "Twenty pounds was stolen out of Mrs Fisher's handbag."

It seemed that Trout had left her bag in the classroom when she went to the staffroom for her coffee and someone had helped themselves from her purse. We were asked if anyone had come into school during playtime and I remembered I had, so I shot my arm up.

"Did you see anything, Joanna?" asked Mrs Horrocks.

"No, Miss," I replied.

Then we all had to go and fetch our bags and coats and tip out the contents. Suddenly, my blood ran cold and I felt a gripping feeling in my bottom! There was a twenty pound note sticking out of one of my plimsolls!

For a split second, I felt like shoving it down into the toe. But it had been spotted by the people around me who gave a great shout and started waving. I went bright red and, as I was led away like a prisoner for further questioning, I caught the hint of a smirk on Darren's face and I knew it was him. He'd planted this on me to get me into trouble and, I couldn't say anything, because I didn't have a shred of evidence to back it up!

Fortunately, Mrs Horrocks didn't think I was guilty, either.

"You've always been such a good girl, Jo," she said, using my short name to show she was on my side. "I can't imagine for a minute you would do a thing like this."

She went on to say that, because the money had been recovered, she'd decided not to involve the police and - best of all - she wasn't going to tell my parents, either.

"Let's just see what happens," she added, rather mysteriously.

Now I thought, in this country, you were supposed to be innocent until proven guilty. Not so at my school. After the stealing incident, everyone started treating me differently. Mrs Fisher was always finding fault with my work and never smiled at me, even though I tried to be friendly. The boys ignored me, including Mark - which I found very hurtful. Only Fran, dear old Fran, stayed my friend.

"Wish we could nail him, smarmy git!" growled Fran, as Darren ran past us with an insolent wink.

The following Wednesday was Mark's birthday. During the holidays, there had been talk of a party, but obviously I wasn't being invited now because all the others were talking about it and I hadn't been asked. Even so, I decided to give Mark the present I'd got for him. It was a lovely pen. He'd never got one and was always borrowing from other people, so I thought he'd be pleased, but he refused it.

"Expect you stole it," he said rudely. I felt as if I'd been slapped in the face. This time, I couldn't stop the tears rolling down my face.

"I don't want to go out with you any more," I snivelled.

"The feeling's mutual!" he replied, coldly.

It took me a while to get over this, but by the weekend I'd persuaded myself that a boyfriend who didn't trust me an inch, wasn't worth having. As I went round to Fran's house on Saturday morning, I saw the school team playing their first match of the season on the field. Normally, I would have stopped to watch, but this morning I just walked on. I did notice, however, that little Nobby Jones was playing. He was sub. Obviously, star player Darren had failed to turn up.

Fran wasn't in when I called. She'd gone to get something with her dad. I resigned myself to a long and lonely day, but, just before lunch, she rang me up.

"Guess what I'm holding in my hot little hand," she chuckled.

"Your first bra?" I joked. "The World Cup?"

"Far more exciting than either of those," she giggled. "A mobile phone!"

Jammy Fran had her own mobile! Her dad reckoned it was an essential safety measure these days. Sensing I was a bit down, she suggested going into town together at two o'clock.

"You need some shopping therapy," she said.

"No money," I sighed.

"Make that window-shopping therapy, then," she laughed.

As we walked to the shops, we talked about Mark.

"You still like him, don't you?" asked Fran.

"No, I don't!" I retorted. "He's a pig."

"You don't mean that," Fran continued, sounding like some Agony Aunt. "I think you two need to talk."

Before I realised what she was up to, Fran had whipped out her mobile phone and dialled Mark's number. His mum answered.

"Mark's not here," she said, sounding a bit narked. "He's out looking for his new bike. It was stolen from our garage this morning."

Fran signed off and we stood looking at each other, very surprised. Mark's new bike was his pride and joy. It was a mountain bike, the latest model, with loads of gears and special brakes. He'd been given it for his birthday and it cost over nine hundred pounds. I'd heard him telling Darren as they cycled past one day.

"Poor old Mark. Bet he's gutted!" exclaimed Fran.

"Serves him right!" I added, trying to sound hard.

We had a nice afternoon mooching around the shops. Fran had enough money for an ice-cream, which we shared.

We were just setting off for home when something caught my eye. There was a bike parked outside a second-hand shop - you know, one of those trade-stuff-in-for-money places that are springing up everywhere. The bike looked very familiar. Then I realised - it was Mark's bike!

Without a word, I grabbed Fran's jacket and yanked her into an alley. She was used to moves like this because we often avoided people we didn't want to meet. When I pointed across the street, her eyes really widened with surprise. Darren had come out of the shop and was clearly trying to sell Mark's bike to the shopkeeper.

What could we do? Here was my proof that Darren was a thief, but he would need to be caught red-handed if anything was going to stick. We thought of confronting him ourselves, but that was a bit dodgy. Darren was obviously a nasty piece of work. We thought of telling the shopkeeper, but he might not believe us, or part with such a bargain. We looked round for a policeman, but like they say, there's never one around when you need one. Then Fran remembered her mobile!

"I'll dial 999!" she whispered.

The police promised they'd send a car round as soon as possible.

So we waited and waited, but nobody arrived. I was beginning to get very agitated. Darren had gone back inside the shop to collect his money and, before long, would be clean away.

"Come on, come ON!" I almost shouted.

"Is something wrong?" asked a familiar voice.

It was Mrs Fisher, the Old Trout! She was passing with her husband, a fat man with a bushy beard who looked like Father Christmas. Hurriedly, we told her the situation. Normally, grown-ups say "slow down" and stuff like that, but she took it all in at once. Then, without a moment's hesitation, she marched across the road.

It all happened in a rush after that.

Darren came out of the shop, looking very pleased with himself, and walked slap-bang into Mrs Fisher! Dropping the money, he ran off. It didn't matter - he was well and truly in the frame now and would get his come-uppance later. We got the bike back and Fran phoned Mark to tell him to come and collect it. Then the police arrived.

I learned later that Mrs Horrocks and the staff suspected Darren of stealing the twenty pounds all along. He'd been expelled from his previous school for theft. Now he was expelled from our school, too.

"Wonder what will happen to him?" mused Fran.

"Don't know and I don't care!" I exclaimed - and this time I meant it!

The whole stealing business was soon forgotton, but two things remained. I had found Mark's bike, but I had lost Mark! He'd gone off me, even though I was totally innocent. We never got back together again, even though Fran tried to engineer it more than once. Life's very unfair, isn't it?

The other thing that stayed with me was Mrs Fisher's immediate help that day. She needn't have bothered with two tiresome little girls from her class. I was grateful the the Old Trout was still a teacher on a Saturday afternoon!

A SPIDER FOR TEA

Mum was in the kitchen, making rock cakes. She makes wonderful rock cakes. They're dark and crunchy on the outside and soft and fluffy on the inside. I sat on a stool, watching her and smiling.

"The answer's no," said mum.

"I haven't asked for anything yet!" I cried.

"You're going to," added mum. "You only ever smile like that when you want something - usually something you can't have."

Of course, mum was right. I wanted a tarantula. I'd seen a programme about them on TV. They're the most amazing creatures, delicate, intelligent and only aggressive when upset. Then I'd read in the paper that keeping reptiles and insects was one of the country's fastest-growing hobbies and I realised I could have one of my own. Wouldn't that be cool? A big, hairy tarantula spider as my pet! I decided to go for it ...

"Well actually, mum," I blurted out. "I want a tarantula."

"The answer's no," repeated mum.

"Aw, come on, mum," I whined. "You haven't even thought about it. What harm would a tarantula do? It'd be in a tank in my bedroom. Nobody would see it except me."

"I'd see it," said mum, putting her wooden spoon down and looking me straight in the eye, "when I make your bed and tidy your mess. And I don't like spiders. The little ones that scuttle across the floor frighten me to death, so I'm not going within half a mile of a big one with hairy legs and fangs. The answer's no, Jo, and that's final!"

I went into a sulk for the next few days, but it didn't do any good. Mum's mind was made up - and she was thinking about other things, anyway.

She'd been invited to put her name forward as a J.P. That means "Justice Of The Peace". They're judges who sit at the local courts, trying petty criminals. It was a great honour for mum. We're not particularly posh, but her friend Mrs Harrison-Parker is, and it was she who got mum involved. This woman was coming round to tea next week to discuss the next stage. I decided to make sure I was out!

The tarantula battle seemed over until, one lunchtime at school, this little kid came up to Fran and me in the playground. His name was Tom and he was a Fourth Year in David's class.

"I hear you want a tarantula," he said.

"How'd you know that?" I asked.

"Your brother told me," he explained. "I've got one. You can buy it if you want."

Tom was moving to a smaller house, so he had to get rid of a lot of his stuff. He had a Mexican Rose tarantula, complete with tank and heat-pad, for sale for only fifteen quid. That was a real bargain!

"I'll take it!" I said.

When the kid had gone, Fran drew my attention to a couple of small matters - where was I going to get the money and where was I going to keep the spider?

"The money's not a problem," I chuckled. "I've got the best part of twenty pounds left over from my holiday and I know where the thing can be kept."

"Where?" asked Fran.

"Round at yours!" I cried.

I expected Fran to object to this idea, but she seemed quite taken with it. She's always up for something different and exciting. That's why I like her so much.

"What about your folks?" I asked, suddenly feeling I'd been a bit pushy. "Do they suffer from agrophobia?"

"Agrophobia, you ignorant child," corrected Fran, "is a fear of wide open spaces. Terror of spiders is called arachnophobia."

"Whatever," I said, shrugging my shoulders.

"Well," laughed Fran, "they don't suffer from either and they won't mind having a tarantula in the house, because they're both out working most of the time and probably won't notice it's there until Christmas!"

So it was that Fran and I found ourselves at Tom's house the following afternoon, buying Madonna.

"Is that what you're going to call the creature?" exclaimed Fran, as we staggered home carrying the heavy glass case between us.

"Tom said it's female," I explained.

"And she's a cool-looking babe in a sexy black outfit with a few lumps and spikes here and there."

"Madonna it is, then!" chuckled Fran.

A few days later, a letter arrived for me. It didn't come in the post - it was pushed under my bedroom door. The words in the letter were all different sizes. It said:

"PaY me 50 PENce A dAY or I BLOW your SECreT"

This was a pathetic attempt at blackmail! I marched next door to David's room.

"You saddo!" I spat. "You couldn't even be bothered to cut the letters out of a newspaper, like a proper blackmail note. You did it on your computer!"

"So?" replied David, holding out his hand. "Pay up - or mum will find out about your little scam!"

I started to see red and felt like hitting his smug, goody-goody face, but I stopped myself. Instead, I grabbed his outstretched hand and led him towards the door.

"Come with me," I said.

"Are we going to get the money?" he asked.

"No," I replied, tightening my grip viciously, so he couldn't escape. "As you're so interested, we're going to see the spider."

"What do you mean?" gasped David, going a bit white.

"Madonna likes to come out of her case," I hissed, menacingly. "She'll crawl all over your hands ... or face!"

David gave a cry of fear and yanked his hand away. He ran into his bedroom, slamming the door.

"Wimp!" I shouted.

Mrs Harrison-Parker wasn't due to visit until Monday afternoon, but mum started cleaning the house on Saturday morning. Honestly, you'd think the Queen was coming to stay for a week! She spring-cleaned the kitchen from floor to ceiling, took down all the net curtains and washed them, tidied out cupboards that had been full of junk for years and that the woman wasn't likely to look into. It was ridiculous! Even dad said so, but he just got a flea in his ear and marched off to the pub, grumbling to himself.

By Sunday afternoon, mum had amassed a huge pile of rubbish and junk in the back garden.

"Fancy coming to the tip with me,

Jo?" asked dad.

"No thanks, dad," I replied. "Got things to do."

It was a lie. I had nothing to do, but I couldn't be seen at the tip with my dad. I used to love going when I was little, reaching up and tipping the rubbish into that great pit with all the other stuff, but I was big now and those days were over. Can't they understand that?

"Okay, then," called dad, sounding a bit disappointed. "I'll take David."

"Good idea," I agreed. "Why don't you leave him there?"

Mum was also out, visiting Gran, so I had the house to myself for a while. I settled down on the sofa and had just found a good film on the Movie Channel when there was a knock on the door. It was Fran.

"Problem!" she said, thrusting forward a cardboard box with holes in the lid. "I can't keep Madonna."

I imagined that her mum and dad had finally woken up to the fact that they were keeping a large, exotic spider. But it wasn't that at all.

"It's Horace," explained Fran, bringing the box inside. "The stupid cat's been watching her ever since she arrived. I never thought he'd do anything, but he did. I heard this crash upstairs and found he'd pushed the tank over to get at her. Luckily he didn't, and she wasn't hurt, but she can't stay, Jo. It'll only happen again."

I was still standing in the hall, wondering what we could do, when the back door opened and mum came in with gran.

"Upstairs, quick!" I hissed, and we shot up to my room like scolded rabbits.

"That's right!" called gran. "Run away the moment I come round to see you!"

"Down in a minute, gran!" I called back.

I was in a terrible panic, but Fran used her brain as usual and stayed cool as a cucumber.

"Put Madonna on top of your wardrobe," she said, handing me the box. "There are other boxes up there, so she won't be noticed. And it's right above the radiator, so it'll be nice and warm."

"She can't stay there ... " I began.

"Of course she can't," cut in Fran. "We'll work out what to do with her tomorrow. But for now, she's safe!"

We went down and chatted to gran as if nothing had happened.

The next morning, we set off to find a home for our unwanted pet. It was the first Monday of half-term, so everyone was in and we tried persuading the likes of Mark and Eddie that they wanted to buy a tarantula. They were having none of it, of course, so I had the brainwave of advertising the whole package - case and all - in the local free-ads.

We went to the office in town and, with the last of my money, paid for an advert in the Pets Section, giving Fran's number. Then we set off for home.

On the way I realised I'd left my purse in the office, but we decided to pick it up another day. There was nothing in it other than my ID card.

Mum was still in tidying mode when we got back to mine for lunch.

"Mrs Harrison-Parker is due at three o'clock," said mum. "So I've had a final look round. I've thrown out all those boxes from the top of your wardrobe, Jo. They look so untidy!"

Fran and I looked at each other, speechless with horror. Then, as quickly as we could without attracting attention, we hurried upstairs. My room had been sorted with military precision and everything mum thought I didn't want had been thrown away. Madonna's box was in a pile just inside the back door, but there was no sign of her inside.

"What do we do now?" I murmured.

"Start looking," replied Fran, grimly.

Now it's hard enough looking for a missing animal when everyone knows what you're doing, but when you've got to pretend you're looking for something else, and your mum is up to ninety-nine about the imminent arrival of a very important visitor, it's nigh-on impossible! As best we could, Fran and I searched under the carpet and behind the sofa, in the cupboards, up the curtains, even under a loose floorboard in the larder - but there was no sign of Madonna. She was probably somewhere very obvious, but we couldn't find her.

"Shall we give up?" asked Fran, wearily.

"We'd better," I answered. "That woman will be here any minute."

Sure enough, a few moments later, the doorbell rang and mum hurried to let Mrs Harrison-Parker in, giving her hair a final pat to make sure it was all in place.

"How lovely to see you, Mrs Harrison-Parker," gushed mum. "Do come in!"

As I said, I planned to make myself scarce while this visit was on, but Fran was fascinated by this upper class woman in her posh outfit with matching bag and shoes and expensive scarf tied casually round her neck.

"Let's watch," she whispered, excitedly.

I thought this was a pretty boring idea, but it didn't turn out like that. Mum and Mrs Harrison-Parker chatted for a few minutes and then mum served the tea. She'd made smoked salmon sandwiches, which cost a fortune, and was serving them in gran's best silver dish, complete with cover.

With a barely disguised flourish, Mum lifted the cover ... and there, sitting on the neat little pile of white triangles, was Madonna! She looked bigger, blacker and hairier than ever before. Mum and her visitor looked at each other for several moments, totally aghast. Then ...

"AAARRRRRRRGHHHH!" they both screamed.

Fran and I were worrried that they'd clobber Madonna with a handbag, so we rushed into the room.

"Don't worry, mum," I cried, emptying some biscuits out of a tin and popping Madonna inside. "We'll rescue you."

"D-D-Do you know anything about th-th-this?" spluttered mum.

"No," I answered, looking wide-eyed with innocence. "Can't imagine how a creature like that got here!"

Just then, there was a knock at the door. Mum answered it. She returned shortly afterwards with a face like thunder. Behind her came the girl from the Free-Ad paper.

"I thought I'd drop this in on my way home," she said, handing me my purse. "You left it behind this morning when you placed that advert for your tarantula."

HANDLE WITH
CARE

A PENNY FOR THE OLD GUY

Uncle Harry is my dad's father's brother - in other words, my grandad's brother. Really, he should be called Great Uncle Harry, but that's too much of a mouthful and it's always been just plain Uncle Harry.

He's a funny old man. Looks like an ape. No, he does, honestly. He's quite small, not much bigger than me, and he's got long arms with big hairy hands on the end. If he sat up in a tree and ate a banana, you'd think you were at the zoo. Anyway, at the beginning of this month, Uncle Harry came to stay with us for a few days.

The old boy hadn't been well lately and needed some kind of test. They couldn't do it where he lived, so he'd come to the hospital near us. Dad was going to take a day off work and go with him. It was okay having him with us. We've got a tiny spare room which he used, so I didn't have to turn out of my bedroom and share with David - that would be awful! Mum cooked some really nice food for a change. The problem with Uncle Harry is that he's deaf, even with his hearing aid.

"Morning, Uncle Harry," I said at breakfast one day.

"Eh?" he replied.

"MORNING, UNCLE HARRY!" I bellowed.

"No need to shout, girl," he snapped.

"Pass the toast, please," I continued.

"Eh?" he said.

"Please would you pass the toast," I repeated, trying not to raise my voice too much.

"Yes, I do like roast," he agreed. "Especially your mum's. She's a very fine cook."

And so it went on. In the end, I gave up trying to make conversation and resorted to just nodding and smiling. He seemed quite happy with that. Maybe the effort of talking was too much for him.

Well, for once I was glad to go to school. Mrs Fisher had organised some group projects which was a way of working we hadn't tried before. The most exciting thing about it wasn't the work, but who you were with. Fran had been picked to work with Mark and I had been paired with Eddie. Poor old Eddie! I could tell he still fancied me by the way he lent me things and talked excitedly about our topic - Farming In The Middle Ages - which he didn't give two hoots about. His work was terrible! He still got his "theres" confused, spelling it "t-h-e-r-e" when it should be "t-h-e-i-r" and vice versa and, worse still, he didn't understand apostrophes. He put them on every single letter 's' he could find, like someone sprinkling confetti at a wedding. I wasn't going to tell him, even though it annoyed me silly. I'm not the teacher, am I?

Still, Eddie was easy to work with and tried very hard because he thought he was pleasing me.

I expected Mark and Fran to rub each other up the wrong way, but that didn't happen. Whenever I looked over at them, they were working happily together or laughing. Fran's wicked sense of humour seemed to appeal to my ex. I couldn't help noticing, with a sick feeling in my tummy, how gorgeous he looked when he was laughing.

Eddie's urgent tugging at my sleeve brought me back to reality.

"You going to the Firework Display on Saturday, Jo?" he asked.

"What Firework Display?" I replied.

"The big one, up at the Golf Club," he explained. "We've all decided not to buy our own fireworks this year and go there instead. It's a tenner to get in, but it's really cool. Massive fireworks!"

"Are you two talking about your work?" called Mrs Fisher. Although I liked her now, the Old Trout could still be pretty 'teachery' at times!

"Yes, Miss," I called back, a bit cheekily. "Eddie's just explaining to me about Medieval Strip Farming."

"Wonders will never cease," she replied.

On the way home, I asked Fran about this big display. She knew all about it and was going with her parents. How come nobody had told me? More to the point, how was I going to get there?

"Mum," I asked at tea-time, "can we go to the firework display on Saturday?"

"No," replied mum. "We'll be taking Uncle Harry home."

"Well, can I go with Fran, then?" I pleaded. "It's only a tenner to get in."

"I haven't got a tenner to spare," said mum. (Of course, she had - but she still hadn't really forgiven me for that spider business.) "If you want to go, you'll have to pay for it youself."

Well, I hadn't got the money and I had no intention of pulling the same stunts that I'd tried when I wanted my tummy button pierced. So what could I do? Fran, as always, knew the answer.

"We'll make a guy," she said.

Of course! Why didn't I think of that? It's the traditional way to raise money for Bonfire Night.

"Your place or mine?" I asked eagerly.

"Mine!" sang Fran, in a put-on weary voice. "My father reads big, fat newspapers and I haven't got a mother like a she-dragon!"

Have you ever tried making a guy? It's not nearly as easy as it looks, especially when you do it on your own. We needed to make a pretty decent one, otherwise we'd get the mickey taken out of us. We bought a cheap mask, which I thought looked pretty scary, and then set about rolling the newspaper into big balls which we stuffed down the arms and legs of some old clothes donated by Fran's dad. The problem was, we couldn't get the two halves to stay together. The moment he was moved, our poor Guy keeled over, or left his legs behind.

"This is HOPELESS!" I shouted, giving the stupid-looking stuffed jumper a savage kick.

"Temper, temper," scolded Fran. "There must be a way ... "

"Yes, there is!" I chuckled, miming a flashing light above my head like a cartoon. "Come with me, my child."

Keeping Fran in the dark, just to annoy her, we hurried back to my house. In the garage, there was a wheelchair that Dad had hired for Uncle Harry. But the old chap was perfectly mobile and wasn't going to use it, so I opened it out and sat in it, assuming a dead still pose.

"You're not serious," gasped Fran, grasping my idea.

"I most certainly am!" I replied, grinning from ear to ear. "In that mask and some of his clothes, I'll be the most lifelike Guy in town!"

It took Fran a while to get used to this idea, but as she wasn't the one making a fool of herself, she finally agreed. And so straight after school on Friday, I sneaked up to Uncle Harry's room and borrowed his old flat cap and long, brown overcoat. He wasn't using them - it was the day of his appointment and he'd gone to hospital with dad. The clothes smelt stale, so I held my breath as I put them on and jumped into the wheelchair, which Fran was holding at the gate.

"If we get caught or laughed at," she exclaimed, "this was your idea!"

We hadn't gone far when we passed this little kid of about six, coming home from the shops with her mother.

"Look, mummy," the girl cried, pointing at me. "That Guy is moving!"

Without thinking what I was doing, I leapt out of the chair and shouted ...

"BOO!"

It frightened the living daylights out of the kid.

"ARRRGHHH!" she screamed.

We had to run away with the mother shouting at us and shaking her fist.

"Nice one, Jo," said Fran. "Earned a lot of money there!"

From then on, I sat as still as I could. We parked ourselves outside the supermarket and were just starting to attract a small, amused crowd and a few pennies, when the manager came out.

"Move along, please," he ordered.

"We don't allow begging outside our store."

Begging? Huh! Doesn't anyone remember the rituals of childhood any more? The same thing happened when we parked outside the station, trying to catch the commuters as they came home. This time, though, it was a policeman who told us off.

"Strictly speaking," he said, in a rather pompous voice, "what you're doing is illegal. But I shan't take the matter any further if you desist forthwith."

"What did he say?" I asked, when he'd gone.

"No idea," said Fran - though I knew she did. "If he can't speak plain English, how can we be expected to understand him?"

We decided to set up our final pitch outside the newsagent just round the corner from my house. Then, if there was any more trouble, we could just bolt home.

But there wasn't any more trouble, well not that sort anyway. Lots of people came in and out of the shop for their evening papers and, chuckling at our unusual-looking Guy, they all threw a few coins into the hat.

"How much now?" I asked from

behind the horrid mask.

"About four pounds, fifty ... and counting," said Fran.

Now I couldn't see very well through that mask and it wasn't until Fran gave me a nudge that I realised something was up. Squinting through the little round eye-holes, I saw a familiar white car draw up right in front of us. It was our car! And out stepped dad, hurrying round to the passenger side to help Uncle Harry out. They had obviously finished at the hospital and were stopping for the old bloke's tobacco on the way home.

There was another cartoon-moment as dad caught sight of us and his eyes nearly came out of his head on stalks. But he was quick-witted enough to say nothing and concentrated on helping Uncle Harry into the shop.

"Shall we scarper?" whispered Fran, when they were safely inside.

"Too obvious," I replied. "Let's sit it out."

I assumed my most rigid and motionless position as dad and Uncle Harry came back out of the shop. I couldn't believe it when the old boy shuffled over and spoke to Fran.

"That's a good-looking Guy you've

got there, dearie," shouted Uncle Harry, dropping a couple of coins into the hat.

"Thank you," said Fran, as bold as brass. "We tried really hard to make him look lifelike."

"He's lifelike all right ... " chuckled the old man, before dad took his arm and yanked him back towards the car.

"Do you think he knew?" giggled Fran, as they drove away.

"Course not!" I laughed, lifting the mask for some much-needed air. "The silly old duffer didn't have a clue!"

By the end of the evening, we'd managed to raise about eight quid. I was sure I could blag another couple of pounds from somebody, so it was mission accomplished!

"I'm really looking forward to this display," I exclaimed.

"Me, too," agreed Fran. "Mark's going to be there."

"So?" I asked, rather too quickly.

"Nothing!" she replied, with the hint of a blush. "I just thought it would be nice if we're all there together, that's all!"

Later, I sneaked indoors and put everything back where I'd got it from. Then I went to get a drink, feeling very chuffed. That soon changed! Dad was waiting for me in the kitchen!

"What do you think you're playing at?" he asked, obviously very angry.

"Nothing, dad," I said.

"You've no right to borrow that wheelchair without asking," scolded dad. "Let alone dress yourself up in Uncle Harry's clothes. They're personal. Could have been money or stuff in the pockets!"

"Sorry, dad," I said, hanging my head.

"You will be," he added. "I want half of the money you made. It'll help pay for the hire of the chair."

I couldn't believe it as dad took four pounds from me the next morning. I moped around, fuming that I wasn't going to be able to make the Firework Display after all. Then it was time for Uncle Harry to leave. As he said goodbye to me, he pressed a folded ten-pound note into my hand.

"Spend it on something you really want," he croaked.

I felt SO guilty! I couldn't refuse the money - the old boy wouldn't let me do that - but, at the same time, how could I take it from him, after all we'd said and done? I decided to confess.

"Uncle Harry," I said, as I helped

him hobble to the car. "I took your clothes without asking."

"Eh?" he said.

"Yesterday, Uncle Harry," I said, much louder. "I borrowed your clothes without telling you."

"Eh?" he repeated.

Then I saw the twinkle in his eye. He was pretending not to hear. He'd known everything all along.

"Bye, Uncle Harry," I said, giving him a kiss on the cheek. "Love you!"

MERRY CHRIS
AS
A.COL
FIZZ

THE CHRISTMAS PARTY

"Mum," I asked, drying the dishes after tea. "Can I have a Christmas Party?"

"Okay," said mum.

"Oh, go on, mum," I continued, whining on automatic pilot ... until I realised what she'd said! I asked her to say it again, just to be sure.

"I said okay, you can have a Christmas Party," repeated mum.

"YES-S-S!" I whooped, punching the air and nearly knocking all the saucepans off the shelf.

It wasn't until mum sat down and started looking through the Yellow Pages for an entertainer that I realised something was wrong.

"Mum," I said, sliding down beside her on the sofa, "what kind of party have you got in mind?"

"Well," she replied, in a business-like fashion, "I thought we could combine it with your birthday and get everything over in one go. You could ask your friends, I could ask the family and David could pay back some of the people he owes. He's been to a lot of sleepovers lately."

There was so much wrong with all this, I didn't know where to start. So I just blurted out ...

"No, mum! I want a PROPER party!"

You see, I'm one of those unlucky people who have their birthday at Christmas. It's on Boxing Day, actually, which isn't quite as bad as having it on Christmas Day itself - but you still lose out. People don't want to buy two lots of presents, especially at this time of year, so they give you one big thing (which usually isn't very big at all.) Fran's birthday is in the summer and she gets loads of stuff then and loads more at Christmas. It's not fair!

Still, never mind that now. Mum had some ghastly gathering in mind, with party games and stuff like that, like when I was six. She needed putting right!

"A proper party, mum," I explained, "is where you have low lights and loud music and play games like Sardines."

"That's a teenage party and you're not a teenager!" she snapped.

"I'm nearly eleven!" I retorted.

"That's a long way from being a teenager," insisted mum. "Now you can have a traditional family party or nothing."

"Then I'll have nothing!" I said, flouncing out.

I told Fran all about this latest conflict as we walked to the sweet shop on the first morning of the Christmas holidays.

"You could have saved yourself all this hassle," she said, throwing a green jelly baby into her mouth. "There's a Christmas party at the Youth Club tomorrow night."

"Really?" I cried excitedly. "Who's going?"

"Everyone!" answered Fran.

"Who's everyone?" I persisted.

"Well, I'm going," said Fran. "And so are you, if you're allowed. That's everyone, isn't it?"

For some reason, I had a feeling that Fran knew more than she was telling me and was covering it up with a joke, but I let it pass.

That afternoon, we called at the Church Hall to ask about the party and, as usual, Damien was in a state. His partner had gone away for a few days, leaving him to look after their one-year-old baby, Daisy. He asked us to take care of her for a while, but we said a polite "no thank you" and offered to prepare for the party instead.

We spent the rest of the day putting up decorations, blowing up balloons and shifting furniture. By the time we had finished, the old Church Hall looked well cool!

The party itself was on Friday evening. So, on Friday morning, I wandered round to Fran's to discuss what to wear. Well, surprise surprise, Fran was in town - having her hair done! I could hardly believe it when her mum gave me the message to meet her outside Marks and Spencers at twelve noon. She duly arrived, about ten minutes late, with her ginger hair cut and shaped into a lovely modern style.

"You look completely different!" I exclaimed.

"I'm not sure if that's a compliment or not," she laughed.

"Oh, it is, it is!" I cried. "You look terrific."

Fran wasn't content to leave it there. As well as the new hair-do, she wanted a new outfit to wear as well.

"You're taking a lot of trouble over

this Youth Club party," I commented, as we trailed round Miss Selfridge for the third time.

"It's about time I bothered," replied Fran, casually.

Eventually, she decided on a light blue mini-dress that suited her perfectly. With some new shoes with a bit of a heel, she looked really grown up. I must confess, I felt a teeny bit jealous.

"You're not a teenager for another two years," I said, in a pretend adult voice. But part of me wasn't joking.

The party started at half-past seven and we made the mistake of getting there on time. To begin with, Fran and I were the only ones there, apart from Damien, who kept rushing around with bowls of crisps and saying "well done" about the decorations every time he saw us.

Eventually, Denice arrived with a couple of girls and a boy from the Comp. She was in with them, now. We were still sort of friends, so she gave me a smile and a wave before sitting down at one of the tables with her friends. This was all pretty boring, so I kept drinking cola to pass the time.

"Your teeth'll drop out," commented Fran, passing me my fifth can.

Nothing happened to my teeth, but I had to nip to the loo pretty sharpish! When I returned, the party had suddenly got started. Mark, Eddie and all the boys had arrived, the lights were down, the music was playing really loud and people were dancing.

"Action at last!" I thought to myself, looking round for Fran. I couldn't see her at first. Then I spotted her ... and I felt the blood rush to my face. She was dancing with Mark! Fran was dancing with Mark! Now I understood. That's why she had taken time and trouble over her appearance for the first time in her life. Mark had asked her to go out with him.

I can't believe what I did next. When the music changed, I pushed my way across the floor and asked Mark to dance. He obviously didn't want to and Fran glared at me with real annoyance for the first time in her life, but I didn't care. I'd always hoped Mark would come back to me, and now, here he was, getting off with my best friend. We danced for a bit and then I broke off, saying I had to go to the loo. It was true - I was bursting. Why had I drunk all that stupid cola?

When I came back, Mark was sitting with Fran at one of the tables.

"May I join you?" I asked, pulling out a spare chair.

"Do us a favour, Jo," said Fran, very sarcastically. "Go away!"

I felt as if I'd been slapped in the face! Fran, who shared everything with me and was always on my side, no matter what, was telling me to go away with a snarl of contempt on her face. This was too much!

"Fine!" I cried, bursting into tears and running away. I blundered across the dancefloor and charged towards the door, just as Damien came in with a trayful of orange juice in glasses. I collided with him head-on, like something out of a 'Carry On' film, and the orange went all down the front of me. I was soaked! Worse still, everyone was pointing and laughing at me. I can truly say, it was the worst moment of my life so far. I just wanted to crawl away and die.

Damien fetched my coat and offered to ring my parents, but I didn't want that.

"I'll walk home and get changed," I said. "It's not far."

"I'm not happy about you walking home alone ... " began Damien.

"I'll go with her," said a kind voice.

It was Eddie. Glad of his chance to

ride to my rescue, like one of those Medieval knights we'd been learning about in our project, Eddie offered to walk home with me.

"Thanks, Eddie," I said, giving him a sad smile. "That's very kind of you."

Eddie tried to chat as we trudged the short distance from the hall to my house, but he could sense I was really upset and stopped talking after a while.

"I'll wait here for you," he said.

"I'm not going back, Eddie," I cried.

"You must, Jo!" he exclaimed, sounding really concerned and serious. "You can't let them know you're hurt. Come back with me."

I thought for a moment. Then I said,

"Okay, Eddie. Back in a tick."

We held hands as we returned to the party. I felt much better, having changed out of my cold, wet clothes. And it felt good having someone by my side again – even if it was only Eddie. I wanted to stop holding hands when we reached the hall, but Eddie wouldn't let me.

"I know you don't really want to go out with me," he blurted out. "I'm not good enough for you, Jo. Never will be. But let me be your boyfriend just for tonight, eh? Just to show 'em."

So, arms round each other, we re-entered the room.

It proved a futile gesture. Mark and Fran had gone and nobody took any notice of us, except Damien who hurried over, welcoming me back with his big toothy smile. I wanted to leave again, but they were just serving the food. Eddie's eyes lit up!

"Come on, Jo," he said, pulling my arm. "Let's get ourselves a burger."

Eddie polished off three in the time that it took me to eat one. And he kept urging me to have more.

"Food's your friend," he said, taking a huge bite out of his roll. "It's always there for you. Never lets you down."

I'd never thought about food like that before. Maybe Eddie was right. Or maybe he was just hungry ... and fat!

Well, it went on to be a pretty miserable Christmas. When the big day finally arrived, I found mum and dad had bought me a CD player - plus some earphones so they wouldn't have to hear the music.

"It cost a fair bit, Jo," said mum. "So it's your Christmas and birthday present combined."

See what I mean?

Boxing Day was worse than Christmas Day. Mum, who always manages to get her own way in some form or another, invited gran and the family round for some cold turkey and salad. And David was allowed to have some of his friends round to play his new computer games. Normally, I would have escaped round to Fran's, but that wasn't an option now. Dad noticed how miserable I was.

"Let's go for a walk," he suggested. "It'll get us out of helping with the clearing up."

It was nice walking round the empty street with dad, looking in at other peoples' Christmases. Were theirs hell, too? It certainly didn't look like it, with all the decorations and pretty Christmas tree lights. But who could tell?

"So you've fallen out with Fran?" said dad, putting his finger straight on the problem. How do grown-ups always know how to do that? Amidst floods of tears, I told dad the whole sad story and he ended up giving me a big cuddle.

"Wish everyone was like you, dad," I whispered.

I saw Eddie once or twice during the holidays. He gave me a CD, which was sweet of him because he hasn't got much money, and I once treated him to the pictures. He put his arm round me and we had a bit of a kiss and a cuddle. He's lovely, Eddie. I realised having someone loyal, who's really on your side, is the most important thing. Fat and funny beats blonde and blue-eyed any day!

The real problem was, I really missed Fran. The holidays were long and boring without her company. In the end, I couldn't stand it any longer and I went round to see her. Her dad answered the door.

"Fran's gone shopping with her mum," he explained, adding mysteriously, "She wanted to buy something special."

I was still wondering what he meant when their car pulled up beside me and Fran jumped out.

"Got something for you, Pig Face!" she chuckled.

Fran had bought me a belated birthday present, a smashing pair of designer tracksuit bottoms.

"I can't accept this ... " I began.

"Course you can," she laughed. "I've finished with Mark. He bored me rigid. All he talks about is football, football, football! I chucked him yesterday!"

"Does this mean we're friends

again?" I asked, my heart lifting in my chest.

"It sure does," cried Fran, giving me a happy shove. "Sorry I was so hateful at that stupid party."

New Year came and went and school loomed again - that awful January morning, cold and dark, when the teachers say things like ...

"There's nothing to disturb you until Easter, so you can get on with lots of work!"

But we still had two days left, so Fran and I walked to the sales in town, just as we had done exactly a year ago.

"Look!" I cried, pointing to some boys on the rec. "There's Mark!"

"SO?" exclaimed Fran.

And we both laughed at the echo of our conversation twelve months ago.

As we sat together in McDonalds, slurping milk-shakes, we went over all the things that had happened last year. There was Old Grumpus, that big cat on the Downs, our tarantula, my holiday adventure and all the trouble with Mark and the boys.

"It's been quite a year," murmured Fran, finishing her milk-shake with such force that people looked round, as the gurgling sounded like water going down a gigantic plughole.

"It certainly has," I agreed. "Wonder what this coming year is going to bring?"

AND THAT'S ONLY HALF THE STORY!

Find out what happens to Jo and her friends during the first six months of the year in this delightful companion volume -

On Sale Now!

ISBN: 1-84161-035-6
Price: £2.99

Old Grumpus

and other stories...

— Gordon Volke —

RR